GRANDMOTHER'S TALES

Story and pictures by

CELIA BERRIDGE

ANDRE DEUTSCH

First published 1981 by André Deutsch Limited
105 Great Russell Street London WC1

Colour origination by Dot Gradations Limited, Chelmsford, Essex
Phototypeset by Tradespools Limited, Frome, Somerset
Printed in Great Britain by Cambus Litho, East Kilbride, Scotland

British Library Cataloguing in Publication Data
Berridge, Celia
    Grandmother's Tales
    I. Title
    823'.914[J]

    ISBN 0-233-97357-5

First published in the United States of America 1981
Library of Congress Number 81-67 104

When Sue and Nicky's mother had to go into hospital, their Grandma came to stay. They were very pleased, because Grandma always brought surprises for them, and gave them little treats, and extra pocket money.

Some things were different with Grandma staying.
Dad made her sleep in his bedroom while he slept on
the sofa, because she was a visitor.

Grandma cooked some extra delicious meals for them. And she let Sue and Nicky eat whatever they liked, so they tried all kinds of nice things mixed together.

Grandma did some
funny things.
She sang loudly
as she worked,

and talked to
all the neighbours,

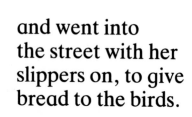

and went into
the street with her
slippers on, to give
bread to the birds.

But best of all, each evening when Dad went to the
hospital to visit their mother, Sue and Nicky got
ready for bed, and then Grandma told them a story.

The first evening, Grandma settled on the sofa and looked around the room for something to remind her of a story. "Dear me, I forgot to put the broom away," said Grandma, "but it reminds me of Pinchglum the witch. Cuddle up, and I'll begin:

Once there was
a witch named
Pinchglum. She had
a black hat, a black
cloak, and a black cat
on a broomstick. She had
fierce yellow eyes; she had
sharp long nails; she had great
big feet; she had long sharp teeth—
and she ate children!
Especially naughty ones.

One day, Pinchglum felt hungry. She took her sack and called her cat. She got on her broomstick and flew across the town. Pinchglum flew over the parks and playgrounds. But the children were being extra good that day—all except one little girl named Brenda.

Brenda was a crosspatch, and that day she was feeling especially bad. She kicked the dog and pinched the baby.

In the end her mother sent her out to play in the yard. So Brenda stomped up and down, shouting and yelling.

Soon Pinchglum heard the noise. She licked her lips.
Down she swooped and opened her sack. 'Help!
Mummy! Help!' shouted Brenda. Her mother looked
out of the window and saw the witch.

She grabbed a broom
and rushed outside.
Brenda was in the sack,
and Pinchglum was just
about to fly away.

Brenda's mother poked
Pinchglum hard, hard in
her bottom with the broom.
'Take that, you witch!'
'Ouch!' yelled Pinchglum,
and dropped the sack.
'Oww!' cried Brenda as
she hit the ground.

Away flew the witch and
was never seen again.
And guess who was not
a crosspatch ever again?"

"I bet she was cross again sometimes," said Nicky. "Grandma, did you just make up that story, out of your head?" Grandma said yes, she often made up her own stories, and she would tell them another one tomorrow.

So the next evening, when they were settled
on the sofa, Sue said, "Tell us a story, Grandma."
"With a happy ending," said Nicky.
Grandma looked around the room, then she began:

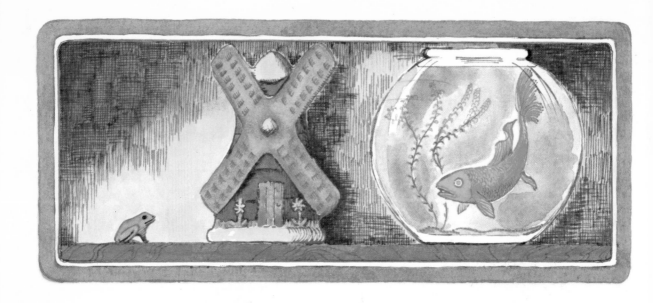

"Once there was a little china frog. He sat on a shelf next to a plaster windmill. On the other side of the windmill there was a glass bowl. A big goldfish swam round and round inside it. How the little frog longed to be in the bowl also, swimming in the cool water. But he was made of china, so he couldn't jump. And the windmill was made of plaster, so it couldn't turn.

The windmill never turned, and the frog never jumped. Only the goldfish moved round and round in his glass bowl.

One day a playful puppy came into the room. She leapt about, barking loudly. 'Rrruff ruff!' She bit the cushions and bounced on the chairs. 'Rrruff ruff!' Then she saw the little china frog on the shelf. 'Rrruff!'

The puppy jumped
up at the shelf,
but it was rather high.
At her first jump,
she knocked the windmill
off the shelf. Smash!

At her second jump, she
bit the china frog by the
leg. Crunch! Then she saw
the goldfish. The puppy
forgot she already had the
little china frog in her
mouth, and jumped again.
She opened her mouth over
the glass bowl and the little
china frog fell into the
water.

Just then a grown up
came in, thank goodness.
The playful puppy was
sent out of the room,
and the broken bits of
windmill were swept away.

The little china frog sat happily in the water,
watching the goldfish swim round and round. But
the big goldfish didn't like having a stranger in his
bowl. Suddenly he rushed upon the tiny frog and
swallowed him at a gulp. This gave the goldfish
terrible indigestion, and two days later he died.
Sadly the children of the house buried him in the
back garden.

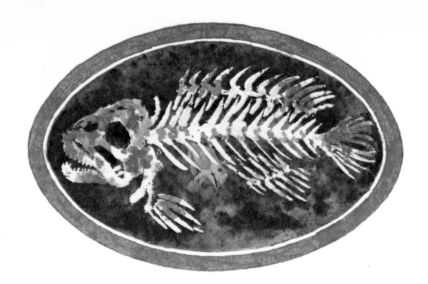

All through the winter, the little china frog lay in darkness under the ground, while the dead goldfish melted slowly into the earth.

Spring came at last, and the children of the house decided to make a pond in the garden, and buy a new goldfish. Their mother fetched a trowel and began digging, to make a hole to put the plastic pond in.

Suddenly she saw something shiny in the earth. It was the little china frog. Hooray! Everyone was very pleased to find him again. They washed him clean in the water of the new pond, and set him among some grasses at the water's edge. When the wind blew, the water lapped over his feet. The little china frog was perfectly happy."

"I thought frogs swallowed fishes, not the other way round," said Sue.
"But the fish was bigger," said Nicky.
"The biggest swallows the smallest," said Grandma.
"But sometimes the smallest one wins, in the end."

The next evening, as soon as they were ready for bed, Sue and Nicky rushed to the sofa for another story. They had been playing on the sofa, and Grandma made them clear away their mess first. Then she began:

"Once there was a poor boy named Jack, who lived with his mother in one room of an old house at the top of a hill. They were too poor to buy toys. But Jack was good at finding things to play with, like lost marbles, and silver paper, and string.

Coming home from school one day, Jack passed a bush with strange shiny seeds on it. He took one home, and put it with his other things, in a box under his bed.

The next morning, at exactly eight o'clock, the seed began to grow. But it didn't grow upwards. It grew great roots which went down, down into the ground, making a hole big enough to climb in.

'I must find out what's down there,' said Jack.
'I'm coming too,' said his mother. Jack took some of
his marbles and silver paper and string. His mother
took a candle, and they climbed into the hole. Down
and down they went, until the roots ended in a
narrow tunnel.

They went along the tunnel until they came to three caves. Jack's mother shone her candle into each one. The first cave led to more tunnels. So did the second one. But the third cave was full of treasure! They filled their pockets with as much treasure as they could carry, and set off back along the tunnel.

Then they heard an awful shout behind them. Some
goblins had come into the caves, and discovered
their loss.
'Run!' said Jack's mother.
'My pockets are too full,' cried Jack.
'Then throw away your marbles,' said his mother.
Jack threw the marbles over his shoulder. They
rolled under the goblins' feet and sent them toppling
in a heap.

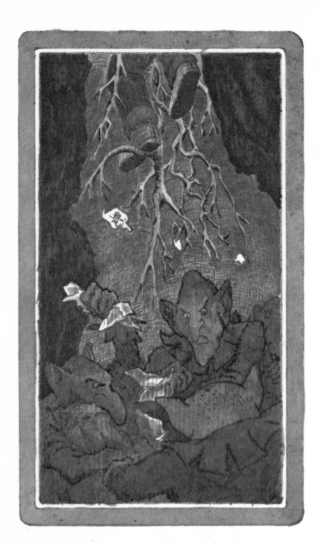

Jack and his mother reached the roots and began to climb. But the goblins were catching up again.
'Quick,' said Jack's mother, 'Throw away your silver paper.' Jack threw it over his shoulder. The goblins thought it was their treasure, and fell upon it greedily. Jack and his mother climbed and climbed. They were nearly at the top when they heard the goblins behind them again.
'Last chance,' said Jack's mother. 'Throw away your string.' Jack threw the string over his shoulder.
'Snakes!' shrieked the goblins as the string entangled them.

Jack and his mother climbed out into their room.
Jack's mother took a big knife and cut through the
roots, which fell away down the hole. Then she
fetched some wood and nailed it up. They were safe.
And when the treasure was counted out, they had
enough to pay the rent and buy all the toys Jack
wanted. And they lived happily for quite some time
after . . ."

"But Grandma, what toys did Jack buy?" asked Nicky.
"I don't know," said Grandma. "But here's a happy thought for bedtime: if you found lots and lots of treasure, what would *you* do?"